Stage Fright

At our table in the cafeteria, Kate speared a bean with each tine of her fork. "But how do you know you'll be in the play?" she asked Stephanie.

Stephanie looked surprised. "I've gotten into every play I tried out for. I was in lots of them at my school in the city."

"Don't you ever get stage fright?" Patti asked.

Stephanie shook her head. "Are you kidding? The bigger the audience, the better I like it." She looked around the table. "I know — let's all sign up for the audition! It'd be neat if we were all in the play together."

**Look for these and other books in the
Sleepover Friends series:**

Starring Stephanie

Susan Saunders

AN
APPLE
PAPERBACK

SCHOLASTIC INC.
New York Toronto London Auckland Sydney

ISBN 0-590-40642-6

12 11 10 9 8 7 6   9/8 0 1 2/9

Printed in the U.S.A.   11

First Scholastic printing, October 1987

Chapter 1

"I don't know if it's this desert movie or Lauren's special dip," Stephanie Green said. "But I'm dying of thirst."

It was Friday night, and all of us were sleeping over at Kate Beekman's house: Stephanie, Patti Jenkins, and me — my name is Lauren Hunter.

"Me, too," I said. "Is there any more lemonade in the refrigerator?"

"Sssh!" Kate answered, her eyes glued to the television set. We were watching a weird old movie on our local cable station. Kate is one of those people who won't talk during a movie, even if it's only on TV. She's a real movie freak.

"Water . . . water . . ." the guy on the screen croaked as he stumbled down a sand dune.

"Doctor Pepper . . . Doctor Pepper . . ." Stephanie croaked, clutching her throat and staggering around.

Patti and I both giggled.

Kate frowned. "Could you wait one second?" she exclaimed. "I just want to see what happens next."

"Kate, we've probably seen this movie five times already," I reminded her. "You know what happens next — there's an oasis on the other side of that dune, and his girlfriend rescues him on a camel."

A strange commercial ended the discussion. "Wanna be in our video?" a voice asked. A tall, skinny guy with spiky, bleached-blond hair and black eye makeup was grinning at the camera.

"Who is that?" Stephanie asked.

"He's part of a new rock group called Boodles," I told her. "They're going to do a video right here in Riverhurst. If you can guess exactly where they're shooting it, they'll let you be in it."

"Really?" Stephanie did a few dance steps. "Can't you just see me on TV?!"

"I'm Russell Gartner," the guy went on. "Stay tuned to this channel for the first of our video clues. And check out our album at the Record Emporium." The Record Emporium is a store at the mall.

"He's definitely cute," Stephanie said thought-fully.

"It's hard to tell if he's tall or short," Patti added. She is the tallest girl in our class, so she worries about that kind of thing.

"For people who were dying of thirst three seconds ago, you certainly recovered fast," Kate interrupted. "Do you want to go downstairs, or not?"

"Yes," the rest of us answered.

Before she opened the door to her room, Kate reminded us, "Quiet! My mom'll kill us if we wake up Dad."

Kate's father is a doctor. He had been on duty at the hospital the night before, and he hadn't gotten any sleep.

"Come on," said Kate. "Watch out for the squeak on the third stair."

I know the squeak on the third stair at the Beekmans' as well as I know the creak in the bathroom door at my house. Kate and I live two houses down from each other on Pine Street. We've been best friends forever, and we've had sleepovers since kindergarten, when it was just the two of us. The summer before fourth grade, Stephanie moved from the city to the other end of Pine Street. She and I got to be friends because we sat next to each other in Mr.

Civello's class. Pretty soon, the three of us — Kate, Stephanie, and me — were spending Friday nights at one another's house.

Kate and Stephanie have never seen everything eye to eye, and I used to find myself caught in the middle. But Patti Jenkins turned up this year in our fifth-grade class. Stephanie and Patti were in the same kindergarten and first grade back in the city, so they've known each other for almost as long as Kate and I have known each other. Patti's a little bit quiet, but very friendly and sensible. Kate and I both liked her right away. Now there are four of us at every sleep-over. My dad dubbed us the Sleepover Friends.

We crept down the hall toward the stairs. Stephanie and I bumped heads in the dark and snickered behind our hands.

"Melissa the Monster's room!" Kate warned in a whisper, pointing at the closed door.

Melissa is Kate's little sister. She's always trying to horn in on our sleepovers, even though she's only a second-grader, so Stephanie and I quieted down fast.

We tiptoed down the stairs. Kate turned on the light in the kitchen and opened the refrigerator.

"There's a whole pitcher of lemonade," she said.

"I'm hungry again," I said, peering into the fridge.

"After fudge, peanut butter and jelly sand-wiches, dip, and taco chips?" Stephanie exclaimed.

"Lauren's the bottomless pit," Kate said. "There's some chicken salad in that green dish. . . ."

"What's this wrapped in foil?" I asked her.

"A fancy dessert for my parents' dinner party tomorrow night," Kate answered. "Chocolate mousse."

She slid the big crystal bowl forward and folded the foil back so we could see. Inside was a dark brown pudding that smelled delicious.

"Mmmm — does that look good!" Stephanie murmured.

Kate examined the mousse closely. "One side is a little higher than the other," she said at last. "Everybody can have a tiny taste out of the high side. Lauren, grab a spoon out of the drawer."

Each of us had a tiny spoonful, just to even out the lopsided mousse. It actually tasted better than it looked, if that was possible — pure chocolate!

"Yummy!" said Stephanie. "As good as I used to have at Alfredo's, in the city!"

Kate poked me. She can't stand it when Steph-anie talks about how many neat things she did when she lived in the city, but I kind of like it.

"It's wonderful," Patti said about the mousse,

5

handing the spoon to Kate. "What are the little purple things in the middle?"

"Crystallized violets." Kate pulled the foil back down over the dessert. "The flowers are dipped in sugar — want to try one?"

"Sure," I answered. I was hungry enough to eat flowers.

Patti and Stephanie nodded.

Kate dug around in the fridge and came up with a small glass jar. "Only four left," she said after she'd unscrewed the top. "One for each of us."

My violet was crunchy and sugary, but otherwise it didn't taste like much.

"They're mostly for decoration," Kate explained. "Okay, who wants lemonade?"

"I do — and let's make some more popcorn in the microwave," I suggested.

By the time we got back upstairs with more snacks, the desert movie was over. Kate snapped the set off. "It's after eleven — WBRM *request* time!"

From eleven to twelve on Friday and Saturday nights, you can call up WBRM, the Riverhurst radio station, and ask them to play a certain record for you — or dedicate a song to somebody you like. Mostly high school kids do it, and it's fun trying to

6

figure out if we know who they are. Once we actually heard a dedication to my brother Roger, who's seventeen. We teased him about it for weeks.

Kate turned her radio on low. Stephanie unzipped her canvas tote and pulled out two small pink boxes. "Guess what I brought?" she said. "Stick-on nails!"

She opened one of the boxes and poured out a handful of plastic fingernails — bright red, of course, because Stephanie's favorite colors are black, white, and red.

"I've never seen any up close," Patti murmured.

For someone who grew up in the city, Patti doesn't know much about makeup or beauty tips or fashion. Stephanie is just the opposite — she's always coming up with new ideas about clothes and style, like wearing her sweatshirt upside down, with the sleeves over a pair of bright tights on her legs instead of her arms.

Stephanie handed Patti five nails, along with the tape that sticks them on. "I'll help you," she said. "Don't touch the glue — it'll stick to anything."

Pretty soon we'd all done our own left hands and were helping each other with the rights.

"Maybe you don't know Boodles yet, but you're going to . . ." a voice announced on the radio.

"It's that guy again — Russell Gartner," I said, sticking some tape on Kate's right thumb and pressing a nail down on top of it.

". . . everybody's going to!" said Russell. "Our rock video's gonna put us at the top of the charts. It's gonna put Riverhurst on the map. . . ."

"Riverhurst *is* on the map, thank you very much," Kate murmured.

". . . and it can make *you* a star, too!" Russell said. "All you have to do is watch for our video clues, then be the first to call this toll-free number. . . ."

A deep voice boomed out "1-800-B-O-O-D-L-E-S." Then Russell Gartner continued.

". . . and tell us exactly where we're shooting our video! Easy, right?"

"Maybe we can guess!" Stephanie said.

"Go to the Record Emporium and check out our album — and free poster!" Russell ordered. "And tune in to Video Trax to find out more about our video clues."

"Wouldn't it be fabulous to do a video? I'd wear my black-and-white jumpsuit," Stephanie decided, "and some sharp dangly earrings —"

"They'd show the tape on Video Trax, and the whole town would see us!" I exclaimed, getting caught up in it.

"And all my friends in the city would, too!" said Stephanie.

Kate shook her head. "It's either someplace that everybody'll guess, like the skating rink, or the mall — or a place nobody'll guess in a million years." She studied the long red nails on both hands. "I wonder how these would look painted with Sunset Pink."

"Sunset Pink?" Stephanie said, completely grossed out. "Really, Kate!"

I finished off the bag of sour cream-and-onion chips and drained my glass of lemonade. "Anybody want more to drink?"

"No, thanks," Patti said.

"Not yet," Stephanie answered. She stretched out her long red nails. "I feel like Alexis Colby."

"More like Queen of the Vampires," Kate said. "I still think they'd look better in pink."

"This next song goes out to Todd S. from Mary Beth Y., with all her love," the WBRM deejay said.

"Too easy," Kate said. "Everybody knows who they are."

Todd Schwartz is a big football star at Riverhurst High, and Mary Beth Young is his girlfriend.

"I'm going to run downstairs for a refill," I said. "I'll be right back."

I was down in the kitchen with my empty glass

9

in a flash. I poured it full of lemonade and set the pitcher back in the fridge. That's when my eye fell on the aluminum foil-covered mousse. I lifted the foil and peeked in — it still looked a little lopsided.

"Nobody'll notice if I take one more tiny spoonful from the back," I said to myself.

I dipped a spoon in the bowl and stuck it in my mouth — fantastic! Carefully, I tightened the foil around the mousse again and hurried upstairs.

I walked into Kate's room just in time to hear the deejay on WBRM say, "To Michael P. of Gaton Lane, from K.S."

"Michael P., Michael P.," I muttered, naturally thinking about kids in high school.

"Gaton Lane!" Stephanie screeched. "That's Michael Pastore's house!"

Michael Pastore is a boy Stephanie likes at Riverhurst Elementary.

"It couldn't be," Kate said. "Fifth-graders doing dedications?" She shook her head.

"Michael Pastore lives on Gaton Lane!" Stephanie practically shrieked. "I ought to know!"

We couldn't argue with that — she definitely should have, because she rode her bike past Michael's house two or three times a week.

"Who is K.S.?" Patti asked. She hasn't been

around long enough to know everyone at Riverhurst yet.

"K.S. — Karen Sims?" I said. Karen is in Michael's room, 5A.

"She's liked Kyle Hubbard since the second grade. What about Karla Stamos?"

"She's probably never heard of WBRM. Karla only listens to classical music," Patti said. "She told me so last week."

Stephanie scrambled to her feet as the music started. "I'm going down to the kitchen," she said. "I need a glass of water."

"Kristy Soames?" I said to Kate.

"She spells it with a 'C,' " Kate replied.

When Stephanie got back upstairs, we'd turned off the radio, but we were still guessing.

"Never mind," Stephanie muttered, her eyes narrowed. "I know who it is."

"Who?" we all asked at the same time.

"It has to be Kathy Simons," Stephanie replied. "I saw her hanging around Michael and some of the other guys at lunchtime this week."

"I never would have thought of her," said Kate. "Last year, any time she even saw a boy she'd run like a scared rabbit. Or a mouse."

"Have you taken a good look at her this year?"

Stephanie wrinkled her nose. "Definitely not mouse-like."

"She looks a lot older," I said. "She could be twelve, at least."

"Kathy Simons." Kate shook her head. "I can't believe it."

"Kate, she actually had on eyeshadow yesterday — it was pale pink, but still!" I said.

"Just because she likes Michael, it doesn't mean he likes her," Patti said comfortingly to Stephanie.

"That's right," Kate said. "And there's always Larry."

Larry Jackson is another boy Stephanie likes. He's in our room, 5B.

Stephanie shrugged. "I've decided you're right about Larry, Kate. His ears *do* stick out too much."

"You're kidding!" Kate was a little shocked. She and Stephanie have been arguing about Larry Jackson's ears for a year.

Stephanie's eyes kept wandering over to the mirror on the back of Kate's closet door.

"What do you think about bangs?" she said, holding her dark, curly hair down over her forehead. Kathy Simons just got a haircut with bangs. "Or I could make a major change — maybe Michael likes girls with short hair."

"I think your hair looks great the way it is," Patti said. "I'm sure it's just a matter of time until Michael notices you."

"If I got on the Boodles video, he'd definitely notice me," Stephanie said. "We have to keep watching those clues."

I made another trip to the kitchen for snacks. So did Stephanie. Even Patti went down once by herself. At about one o'clock, Kate said she was going to pop more popcorn in the microwave. But she was back almost immediately.

"All right, you guys!" Kate said sternly. "Who did it?"

"Did what?" we asked.

"Ate the mousse!" Kate growled.

Chapter
2

The mousse? I had only taken a little more from the high side, I thought. But suddenly I wasn't feeling too well.

"Uh — I took a couple of bites," I admitted.

Stephanie spoke up behind me. "I had a small spoonful or two myself."

"Er . . . I d-did, too," Patti stammered, blushing bright red.

Kate clicked her long red nails together. "So did I," she confessed. "And now we're in big trouble."

"What do you mean?" I asked.

"There's a big, fat pothole in one side of the mousse," Kate answered.

"Why don't you just smooth it out?" Stephanie suggested.

"Smooth it out?" Kate groaned. "The hole is the size of Lake Erie!"

"We'll make another mousse," Patti said quickly. Sometimes we do cook things at sleepovers — but it's always things like grilled-cheese sandwiches or fudge balls, never chocolate mousse.

"Just like that?" Kate shook her head. "Mousses aren't the easiest things to make — Mom worked all morning on this one."

"We have most of the night left," I pointed out.

"Let's take a look at it," said Stephanie.

The four of us crept downstairs again and into the kitchen. Kate took the crystal bowl out of the refrigerator and pulled off the foil. She was right about the hole — if we moved enough mousse from the other side to fill it in, there would be only about an inch of it covering the bottom of the bowl.

"Hmmm," Stephanie said. "I guess your mom would notice."

"You bet she would," said Kate. "There's supposed to be enough here to feed eight people."

"Do you know which cookbook your mother used?" Patti asked, checking the titles of the books on the shelf next to the stove.

"The one on the end," Kate told her. *"Glorious Desserts."*

Patti found a recipe called "Sinfully Delicious Chocolate Mousse," and started to read in a low voice. "We need six eggs," she said, "half a pound of sweet chocolate, heavy cream, and sugar."

"See?" said Stephanie to Kate. "Only four ingredients — it can't be so hard to make."

"Hah!" said Kate. "But I guess it's our only hope," she admitted.

"First we have to melt the chocolate," Patti directed.

It turned out that Mrs. Beekman had bought a pound of sweet chocolate and only used half of it. We put the other half in a saucepan and set it on the stove. It didn't take long to melt into a dark brown puddle — simple. Kate punched a button to turn off the burner.

"Now we separate the eggs," Patti told us.

"What does that mean?" Stephanie asked.

"It means put the yolks in one bowl and the whites in another," I answered. "I've seen my mother do it."

"Good," said Kate, handing me a carton of eggs. "You can show us."

"Take off your nails first," Patti advised.

I pulled them off and piled them on the counter.

Separating eggs looks so easy whem Mom does

16

it: crack the eggshell on the edge of a bowl and pull it open just enough to let some of the white run out. Then pour the yolk back and forth from one half of the shell into the other half. All the white is supposed to come off the yolk and fall into the bowl. Then you dump the yolk into another bowl.

But when I did it, it didn't work out quite that way. On the first egg, I broke the yolk when I cracked the egg. "Sorry," I said. "Guess I hit it too hard."

We threw it out.

I cracked the second egg. The yolk tore on the edge of the eggshell. The yellow ran into the white. We threw that one out, too.

On the third egg, I only got half the white into the bowl — the rest oozed onto the counter. So far we had one yolk, and half a white.

"If this keeps up, we're going to run out of eggs," Kate warned.

"Let me try it," Stephanie said, pulling off her own plastic nails.

She tapped an egg on the edge of the bowl — the shell broke neatly in half. In a second or two, she had it neatly separated. In fact, she separated all six eggs with no problem.

"You ought to be a cook when you grow up," Patti said admiringly.

"Are you kidding?" Stephanie grinned. "I'm going to *have* a cook when I grow up!"

"What's that burning smell?' Kate interrupted.

"The chocolate!" Patti squeaked, jerking the saucepan off the stove with a potholder.

Kate had punched the wrong button on the stove. We stared into the pot. The chocolate was a hard, dark-brown mess.

"That does it," Kate said gloomily. "There's no more chocolate."

"What about these?" I pointed to a glass jar full of Hershey's Kisses.

"They might work . . ." Kate said.

"Sure!" I told her. "The mousse might even be better."

But we weren't home safe yet. Have you ever tried to cook egg yolks without turning them into hard little lumps? It's not easy. You stir and stir, and then you throw all the yolks out because they're not smooth enough.

"What time is it?" Stephanie asked, separating six more eggs.

"Two-thirty," Patti answered, trying not to yawn.

"I guess we won't be having omelettes for breakfast after all," I said sadly. Even Patti glared at me.

We started all over.

Stephanie finally solved the problem of lumps by pouring the cooked yolks through a strainer, which trapped all the hard little bits.

"Now for the whites," Kate said, looking into the bowl doubtfully. "They're so slimy."

Patti checked the recipe. "We use an electric beater to do this part. We'd better close the door. This thing makes a lot of noise."

"Thank goodness!" Stephanie said. "My arm's about ready to fall off from stirring the yolks."

Kate stuck the beater into the bowl of whites and turned it on. First the whites got bubbly, then foamy, then they started to look like shaving cream.

"Do you think the bowl is too small?" Patti asked.

"Everything else is dirty," Kate said, the blades whirring away.

The whites got bigger and bigger.

"Better stop," Stephanie warned. "They're going over the edge. . . ."

Kate jerked the beater out of the bowl without turning it off. *Splat* — foamy white blobs all over the place! They were sliming down the wall, down the curtains over the sink, down the front of the cabinets. Patti had sprouted a puffy, white unicorn horn.

"Neat, Kate," Stephanie said.

By about four A.M., we were done. We'd stirred

the chocolate and cream and yolks and whites together, and poured our mousse into the crystal bowl
on top of the old mousse.

"It looks great!" Patti said.

"Your mom will never know," Stephanie told
Kate.

"Doesn't taste too bad, either." I licked some
mousse off a spoon.

"Don't start, Lauren!" Kate said.

"Just testing," I replied.

"It's kind of two-toned," Patti said.

Kate sent Patti and me outside to look for violets — there's a big patch of them under the pines.
"We can use a few of the old ones, but three of them
are broken. So we'll just have to dip some fresh ones
in sugar and hope they look okay."

Kate handed us a flashlight. She warned us not
to turn it on until we were behind the garage — just
in case her parents happened to be staring out at their
backyard at four A.M.

It's very dark at that time of the morning. Patti
and I walked carefully across the lawn, trying not to
make any noise. That's when I saw it.

"Wow! Look at that!" I whispered to Patti.
"There's a light on in the old McBride house!"

The back of the McBride yard runs into Kate's

20

backyard — and mine. "The house has been empty for as long as I can remember," I whispered. "Somebody mows the lawn once in a while, and somebody painted it last year. But I've never seen a light on in the middle of the night before."

We were looking up at the McBride house, not watching where we were going. Patti bumped right into the Beekmans' big metal garbage can. It tipped sideways, and the lid fell onto the driveway with a clang.

"Oh, no!" Patti gasped.

"Maybe nobody heard," I said.

We darted behind the garage, holding our breath and hoping. But Kate's little sister, Melissa, has the sharpest ears in town.

"Who's out there?" she yelled from her window.

The light in the McBride house switched off — and the lights in Kate's parents' bedroom came on.

"Kate?" I heard Mrs. Beekman call out.

I knew we were doomed.

Patti and I raced back into the kitchen, but Mrs. Beekman had beaten us to it.

"Oh, my stars!" she moaned. "What a mess!"

"Ick-o!" said Melissa, who was right behind her.

There were eggshells all over the counter, a pan full of burned chocolate on the stove, puddles of yellow yolks beginning to dry everywhere, egg whites spattered on the wall, dirty bowls and measuring cups and spoons in the sink, on top of the refrigerator — there was even one on the floor.

"We'll clean it all up, Mrs. Beekman," Stephanie said. She was up to her elbows in soapy water, washing things. Kate was drying.

"Please go back to bed, Mom. By the time you're ready for breakfast, the kitchen'll be spotless," she promised. "You won't be able to tell we were here."

"But what are you cooking in the middle of the night?" Suddenly Mrs. Beekman shrieked. "Did one of you cut yourself?" she asked. She squinted at each one of us. "Kate! There's blood on your arm!" she gasped.

Kate must have leaned her arm against the counter while she was cleaning up. A pile of red stick-on nails was glued to her sweater. Before she could say anything, Mrs. Beekman was shouting, "Morris! Come quickly — Kate's hurt!"

That brought Dr. Beekman downstairs in a flash, carrying his doctor's bag and tripping over the hems of his pajama bottoms. (Dr. Beekman's a little short.)

By the time we'd explained about the nails, and the mess, and the mousse, it was almost five in the morning. Melissa was thrilled that she'd managed to crash our sleepover. But Dr. and Mrs. Beekman were definitely grumpy as they trudged back upstairs to bed.

"I want this place so clean by the time I come down in the morning that this will all seem like a bad dream," Mrs. Beekman warned as she walked out of the kitchen.

"The violets?" I reminded Kate when all was quiet again.

"Forget the violets. We have tons of cleaning to do. I don't think my mother thought too much of our mousse anyway."

Two hours — and two loads of dishes and two moppings — later, the kitchen looked okay. Kate, Stephanie, Patti, and I collapsed at the kitchen table.

"I guess it's too late to go to bed," Stephanie groaned.

"Or too early," Kate said. "Want some breakfast? We could still make some scrambled eggs. . . ."

"NO!" the other three of us yelled.

I never wanted to see another egg, or chocolate kiss, or violet petal again.

Chapter
3

We were so worn out Saturday morning that I forgot about the McBride house for a while. When I got home I went right to bed to nap for a few hours.

But I remembered during lunch, and I asked my parents about it. "I saw a light on in the McBride house last night. Has somebody finally moved in?"

Mom shook her head. "Not that I know of. Gerry?" She looked at my father.

"Maybe the painters left it on when they were there," he suggested.

"They were there months ago. And they only painted the outside of the house, not the inside. Besides," I told him, "while I was staring right at it, the light went off."

"Really?" my mother said. "What time was this?"

"Oh — around four o'clock this morning," I mumbled.

"Lauren! No wonder you look so tired!" said my mother.

"Are you sure 'sleepover' is the right word?" Roger stuck in. "There doesn't seem to be any 'sleep' involved. The 'Sleepless Friends' would be more like it."

I ignored him. Well, first I sneered at him, then I ignored him. "Do you think somebody could have broken into the house?" I said to my parents.

"I guess it's possible," my father replied. "I'll mention it to Tom Warner."

Officer Warner is one of the policemen who patrol our part of Riverhurst.

"And I'll check around the neighborhood," Mom added. "I'm sure there's an explanation, Lauren."

Later that afternoon, Stephanie called to ask if I wanted to go for a bike ride.

"Sure. Have any place special in mind?" I teased.

"Very funny. I thought we could just go over to the mall, okay? Call Kate, and I'll call Patti. Meet you at my house at two-thirty."

Gaton Lane, where Michael Pastore lives, is right on the way to the mall. It's also usually a quiet street. That afternoon, though, the four of us could hear a real racket as soon as we turned the corner.

"Come on, come on — put it right here!" someone shouted.

"Easy out!" somebody else yelled.

Crack! There was the sound of a bat hitting a ball.

"A baseball game!" I shouted. I'm pretty good at sports, and baseball is one of my favorites. I started playing catch with Roger when I was about five.

"I've got it . . . I've got it. . . ."

"He dropped it — run!" a boy called out.

"The sun was in my eyes!" someone whined.

"They're playing in the vacant lot," Stephanie said, braking her bike for a closer look. "There's Michael!"

Michael was there, and so was a whole bunch of other guys: Mark Freedman and Henry Larkin from our room, Kyle Hubbard from 5A, Tommy Brown from 5C, some fourth-graders, even some third-graders.

"Hey, Lauren! Come catch for us — Martin is the pits!" Tommy said when he saw us.

Tommy was in Mr. Civello's class last year with Stephanie and me. Martin Yates, a fourth-grader, is Tommy's cousin, so I guess he felt he could say whatever he wanted about Martin.

"Then Patti's on our team," Mark declared.

Patti's even taller than I am. Normally, she's kind of klutzy, but when she's not thinking about herself, she's great. She can run fast, and she's a really good hitter.

"Kate, too," Kyle Hubbard said. He and Kate were friends because they sat next to each other in fourth grade.

"Do you want to play?" I asked Kate and Stephanie.

Kate shook her head. "Three days of gym a week are plenty for me."

Kate doesn't really like sports, and she hates to get dirty.

Any other time, Stephanie would have agreed with Kate. She doesn't like to get messed up, either. And that day she was wearing a brand-new red, white, and black sweater. But I guess she was willing to risk even sweat and dirt for a few minutes with Michael Pastore.

"Let's play," she said. "Just for a minute. Ple-e-e-ease, Kate?"

Kate rolled her eyes. "Oh, all right!"

We pushed our bikes over the curb and leaned them against a tree. Martin threw me the catcher's mitt.

"Martin, you play third," said Tommy, who was pitching. "Pete can be in the outfield." There were five kids on Tommy's team counting Tommy himself: Henry Larkin, Mark's little brother Jason, Martin, and Pete, the third-grader who'd dropped the ball when we first rode up.

Michael Pastore was on Mark's team. So Stephanie announced, "I'll be on Mark's team."

"You can't," Mark said. "With Patti and Kate, I've got seven. Tommy's only got six with Lauren."

"You can be an outfielder along with Pete," Tommy told Stephanie. "There's an extra glove somewhere."

"Let's go — batter up!" Mark called out. His team was at bat, and he was already on second base.

I hunched down behind home plate. Tommy's a pretty good pitcher. He struck out Andrew, a third-grader, one-two-three. Kyle batted next. On the second pitch, he hit a grounder between first and second. Pete held onto the ball this time, threw it to first, and Kyle was out, too. But Mark made it to third base. He was ready to race home.

Now it was Michael's turn at bat. Michael is short and stocky. When he hits a baseball, it really goes.

"Move farther back!" Tommy shouted to his out-field.

He wound up and really burned one across the plate. Michael swung at it and missed. The ball hit my glove with a *thwock*.

Tommy grinned. "Strike one!"

Michael tapped the plate with the tip of his bat and got into position again. Tommy threw a ball that curved away just as it reached the plate.

"Strike two!"

"Way to go, Tommy! One more and he's out!" Henry was playing first base.

But on the third pitch, Michael's bat and the ball connected. It was a high fly to left field — exactly where Stephanie was standing.

Michael dropped his bat and raced toward first. The ball flew higher and higher. Stephanie squinted up at the sky. She moved under the ball as it started to drop. Her glove was out . . . then the ball seemed to slip through her fingers.

"Oh, no!" Tommy groaned.

Mark had already crossed home plate. Michael rounded second and was headed for third.

"Throw it!" Martin shouted to Stephanie.

Stephanie was fumbling around on the ground

for the ball. She finally picked it up, drew her arm back, and let it fly — and she missed Martin by a mile!

One thing Stephanie can do is throw. At the dunking booth at the school fair, she knocked Mr. Civello into the water about twenty times.

"Just great!" Tommy grumbled as Michael jumped up and down on home plate. "Why did she have to be on my team?"

"Way to go!" "Home run!" "Two-zip!" Michael's team shouted.

Kate batted next, and Tommy struck her out — she's a little nearsighted and doesn't like to wear her glasses. But Mark's team was still leading by two runs.

"Terrific play!" Tommy growled at Stephanie as she came in from the field.

"Sorry," Stephanie said. But she didn't look very sorry.

"You did it on purpose, didn't you?" I whispered.

Stephanie raised her eyebrows. "Lauren!"

It was a good game, but our team couldn't seem to catch up. When Patti knocked in two runs in the fourth inning, it was all over. We didn't get another chance at bat, because Martin and Henry had to go home.

"Martin!" His mother stopped her car at the curb and leaned out the window. "You promised to clean out the garage before dinner."

"Aw, Mom. . . ."

"Henry, your mother is looking for you, too," Mrs. Yates added.

"We'd better go," Kate said, checking her watch. "It's almost five."

"Okay — game's over," Tommy announced glumly.

"We knocked their socks off," Michael said, grinning at Patti.

Patti smiled shyly. Stephanie frowned. She frowned a lot more when she saw who was crossing the street on a bike: Kathy Simons.

"Hi, Mark, Kyle. Hi-i-i, Mi-i-ichael."

"Hi," Michael replied.

Kathy was wearing a pink sweatshirt with gray lines and blue triangles on it, blue sweatpants, and hightop pink sneakers. Everything looked brand-new.

We were hot and sweaty from the game. Stephanie glanced down at the big streak of dirt across the front of her sweater and scowled.

"Hello, Kathy," Kate said pointedly, since Kathy hadn't even bothered to speak to us.

"Oh, hi." She barely nodded in our direction. "Michael, can you take a look at my bike chain? I think it's loose." She shrugged helplessly. "I don't know how to fix it."

"Can you believe her?" Stephanie hissed as we walked to our bikes.

"What about you?" Kate asked. "*You* threw the ball away just to make Michael look good."

"I did not!"

"I saw you do it," Kate said.

"You're not wearing your glasses, and I was all the way out in left field," Stephanie huffed.

"We all saw you. You can throw a lot better than that, Stephanie."

I nodded. Kate was right, of course.

"The sun was in my eyes," Stephanie said, borrowing Pete's excuse for dropping the ball.

"The sun was behind you," I said.

"Oh, what difference does it make?" Stephanie said angrily. "Look at Michael!"

Michael was kneeling down next to Kathy's bike, adjusting the chain. Kathy Simons was leaning so close that their heads were almost touching.

Tommy and Kyle and some of the other boys

waved goodbye, but Michael didn't notice we were leaving.

"He really likes her!" Stephanie said as we rode up the street. "I can't believe it."

"Kathy Simons is a dope," Kate said. "If Michael Pastore likes her, then he's a dope too."

"I think he's just being nice, Stephanie," Patti said in her soft voice. "Michael is very nice."

It was too late to go to the mall. We turned onto Clearview Crescent, which is the street behind Pine Street. It is also the street the old McBride house is on.

"Hey — I forgot to tell you!" I said suddenly. "I think somebody was in the old McBride house last night."

"Lauren, nobody's been in the McBride house for years," Kate said.

I shook my head. "There was a light on on the second floor — Patti and I saw it when we went to look for more violets."

Kate said just what my father had said. "The painters probably left it on."

"Then why did it go off while I was staring at it?" I argued. "Patti saw it, too."

"Actually, I didn't see it go off," Patti admitted. "That's when I ran into the garbage can."

"You know," Stephanie said, "I've been reading a book about ghosts and poltergeists. Most spirits prefer to live in private places — I mean ones with no humans. Do you think the McBride house is haunted?"

Kate rolled her eyes. "You're starting to sound like Lauren," she said.

But no one objected when I suggested that we investigate. We stopped our bikes in front of the McBride house and took a good look at it. The trim had been repainted, and the eaves, too. But a lot of the windows had boards across them, and some of the panes were broken. Shingles were missing from the sides of the house, and a dead branch dangled off the roof. A broken birdbath leaned over in the dry grass.

The sun was starting to set, and some of the windows in the house glimmered with the light from its rays.

"You probably saw a reflection in the window pane, from a streetlamp or something," Kate said to me.

"I know what you're thinking," I told her. "You're thinking that I'm letting my imagination run away with me again. But there's no streetlamp in the backyard. And I know what I saw. I'm going to keep an eye on this place."

"It's kind of spooky." Patti shivered.

"I'm freezing," Stephanie said. It was cold in the long shadows of the house and trees.

"So, how am I going to get Michael Pastore to notice me?" Stephanie asked before we all started home.

"I'm sure you'll think of something," Kate said.

Chapter 4

It wasn't long before Stephanie had it figured out. "It's perfect!" she shrieked as she dropped her lunch tray at our table.

"What's perfect?" I asked. It was Wednesday, franks-and-beans day in the cafeteria. I knew she wasn't talking about lunch.

"The fifth-grade play!" Stephanie replied. "If I'm in it, Michael will have to notice me!"

Every year the four classes of fifth-graders at Riverhurst Elementary put on a play in a special school assembly. Just before lunch that day, our teacher, Mrs. Mead, announced, "This year's fifth-grade play is called *The Woman in Blue*. It's more than a hundred years old — "

The class groaned. "A hundred years old?"

"Mrs. Mead, can't we do something a little more modern?" Sally Mason asked.

"Maybe something about a rock star," Henry Larkin suggested.

"*The Woman in Blue* will be lots of fun." Mrs. Mead ignored the interruptions. "It's a melodrama — lots of action, with a silly heroine who is almost too good to be true and a hero who is also very upstanding. He tries to save her from a terrible villain. . . ."

"Heh, heh, HEH!" Mark Freedman laughed nastily, twirling the ends of an imaginary mustache.

"That's right, Mark." Mrs. Mead smiled. "There is even a ghostly woman in blue. I have copies of several of the scenes." She passed them out to the class. "Please take a look at these. If you'd like to try out for one of the parts, sign up on the list posted on the hall bulletin board. Auditions are next week."

Stephanie sits in the front row in our class. As soon as she got her copy of the play, she started reading.

"I can't think of anything worse," Kate said to me. She and I sit next to each other in the second row.

"Just the idea of being on stage gives me a stomach ache," I agreed.

"Quiet, please, class," Mrs. Mead said. She must

37

have heard us, because the next thing she said was, "There are many other ways to get involved in the play, too: as stagehands, set designers, painters, lighting people, or assistants to Mr. Coulter, who will be the director." Mr. Coulter is the music teacher at Riverhurst Elementary.

"There's a second list on the bulletin board for those of you interested in the production end of things. We can use all the help we can get," Mrs. Mead said before she dismissed us for lunch.

At our table in the cafeteria, Kate speared a bean with each tine of her fork. "But how do you know you'll be in the play?" she asked Stephanie.

Stephanie looked surprised. "I've gotten into every play I tried out for. I was in lots of them at my school in the city."

"Don't you ever get stage fright?" Patti asked.

Stephanie shook her head. "Are you kidding? The bigger the audience, the better I like it." She looked around the table. "I know — let's all sign up for the audition! It'd be neat if we were all in the play together."

"Not me," Kate told her. "I'm going to be an assistant to Mr. Coulter — it'll be good experience." Kate is thinking about being a movie director after college.

"Me, either," I said. "One look at all those people, and I'd forget everything."

"You'll audition, won't you, Patti?" Stephanie
coaxed.

"I'm sure I'd be awful," Patti replied uneasily.

"Come on — it would be good for you," Stephanie insisted. "Help you get over your shyness, right?"

"Well . . ." Patti stalled. She looked kind of
queasy.

"She really doesn't want to, Stephanie," Kate
said.

"Just sign up, Patti — we can practice at the next
sleepover," Stephanie suggested. "Then, if you still
don't want to try out, you can always erase your
name." She gazed at Patti hopefully.

"Oh, all right," Patti agreed at last.

"Great!" Stephanie said. "You're going to love
it!"

The sleepover that Friday was at Patti's house.
Mr. Jenkins was going to drive us to Mimi's Pizza for
dinner, so Kate and I rode our bikes to Patti's house
at five-thirty.

Before we even had time to knock on the front
door, Patti and Stephanie had opened it and rushed
out onto the porch.

Patti started apologizing in a nervous whisper.

"I'm really sorry. If I'd known he was going to be here, I would've called off the sleepover."

"Known if who was going to be here?" I said.

"Lester," Stephanie replied in a low voice. "He's Patti's cousin."

"So?" Kate reached for the doorknob.

"You'll see," Stephanie replied meaningfully.

The lights were off in the living room. We were heading for the stairs when two dark shapes leaped out from behind the couch with a shout: *"Haieee-hah!"*

"Aaaah!" Kate and I screamed together. We both jumped a mile.

A kid spun around on the rug and kicked the air in front of our noses.

"Lester," said Stephanie.

Patti sighed and switched on the lights. "And Horace." Horace is Patti's little brother.

"Hah!" Lester said again, chopping the air with his hands a few times. He was shorter than Kate and skinny, with buck teeth and brownish hair like straw that stood up in back. He had a white handkerchief tied pirate-style around his head. "Scared you, didn't I?"

"Haieee!" said Horace, imitating his older cousin.

40

"Boys, please don't bother the girls." Mrs. Jenkins waved to us from the kitchen. "Hello, Lauren, Kate. Patti's father will be home in a little while." Both of Patti's parents are professors.

"What's with the Karate Kid routine?" Kate asked as we climbed the stairs to Patti's room.

Patti shrugged. "In the last two hours we've had the Incredible Hulk, GI Joe, and cowboys and Indians. I think Lester watches too much TV."

"How old is he?" Kate asked.

"Eight and a half," Patti replied.

"You mean Melissa's going to be like this next year?" Kate groaned. "That's just great!"

"Where'd Lester come from? And what's he doing here?" I asked.

"He lives in the city. My uncle Marvin had to fly to California on business, and he took my aunt Judy with him for a few days. So we're stuck with Lester for the whole weekend."

"Nice . . ." Kate said.

We found out exactly how nice at Mimi's Pizza. The seven of us sat at the long table near the back: Mr. Jenkins, Horace, and Lester on one side, Patti, Stephanie, Kate, and I on the other. Mrs. Jenkins had to go to a meeting at the university. After we'd ordered our drinks and an extra-large pizza with every-

41

thing except anchovies, we girls and Mr. Jenkins picked up our salad plates to go to the salad bar.

"This is a restaurant. You boys behave yourselves," Mr. Jenkins warned Lester and Horace.

"Aye-aye, sir!" Lester replied, saluting Mr. Jenkins.

The salad bar is at the front of the restaurant. There were several people ahead of us in line. Also, there's so much stuff to choose from that it takes a while to make up your mind. By the time we got back to our table with the salads, the drinks were already there. The pizza was cut into slices and waiting on our plates; the boys were halfway through the slices in front of them.

"How is it?" Mr. Jenkins asked them.

"Great!" they said. Both of them were grinning as if they really meant it.

Patti and Kate were sprinkling oil and vinegar on their salads.

"The pizza looks yummy!" Stephanie said.

"Mmmm," I agreed.

Stephanie and I picked up our slices and took big bites.

"Aaagh!" The pizza tasted as if it had been dipped in chili sauce. Flames could have been shooting out of my mouth!

"H-h-h-h-h-otttt!" Stephanie squawked, fanning her mouth with both hands.

We both grabbed our drinks and gulped.

"Yuck!" I almost choked. The soda was so greasy I could hardly swallow.

Lester and Horace had been watching Stephanie and me like hawks. Now they started to smirk and snicker.

Tears were running down my face. Patti handed me her soda. "Here! Drink this!"

Before I took a sip, I held the glass up to the light and peered at the dark liquid. There was a big blob of gold-colored oil floating in it!

"Olive oil," I croaked, still trying not to gag.

"There's red pepper sprinkled all over the pizza," Kate reported, examining her slice closely.

Patti pointed to the jar of red pepper flakes on our table — it was more than half empty.

Lester and Horace were hysterical, giggling their heads off!

Chapter
5

"Apologize to Lauren and Stephanie — right this minute!" Mr. Jenkins thundered at Lester and Horace.

"I'm sorry, Lauren. Sorry, Stephanie," Horace said quickly. Horace is usually an okay kid.

"Well, Lester?" Mr. Jenkins said.

"Aw, Uncle Phil . . . it was just a joke," Lester whined.

Mr. Jenkins glared down the table at his nephew. "We're waiting."

"Sorry," Lester mumbled, staring at his plate.

"Go sit in the car until we're done, both of you," Mr. Jenkins ordered. "You're in big trouble."

Lester and Horace had to wait outside in the Jenkinses' station wagon until we'd ordered another

44

pizza and more drinks and finished our dinner. When we got back to Patti's house, Mr. Jenkins sent them straight upstairs to Horace's room.

"Why can't we watch TV, Uncle Phil?" Lester argued. " 'Hurricane Smith' is on."

"No TV!" said Mr. Jenkins. "I want you both in bed — with the lights out — in ten minutes."

Lester stamped upstairs. Horace was next, with Mr. Jenkins behind him.

"Dinner was gruesome! You'll probably never forgive me!" Patti said anxiously.

"Dinner was okay — Lester was awful," Kate corrected.

"He's gone to bed. He won't bother us any more," I said.

"And we go home tomorrow morning. I feel sorry for you," Stephanie said to Patti. "You have two more days of him."

"Be sure to check out your food before you eat anything," I advised her. My mouth was still sore. I don't think I'll ever forget the taste of oily soda and peppered pizza.

The four of us flopped down in front of the TV set in the Jenkinses' living room. Stephanie clicked on the remote control and switched channels. "Hey, look — it's Russell Gartner, from Boodles."

45

"I'm sure you fans have already seen our first video clue, since we've been running it for days," Russell Gartner was saying. "But in case you haven't, here it is again."

"Video Clue #1 — Boodles" flashed on the screen. Then the letters disappeared, and we were looking at a big room painted white with black spots.

"Polka dots — think how neat they would look with bright red furniture!" said Stephanie. "Or my jumpsuit and red earrings. A play *and* a rock video — Michael would definitely notice."

There was no furniture in the room on the screen — it was completely empty.

"It looks sort of like my old apartment building," Patti said.

"How can you tell?" I asked.

"The fancy trim around the windows and the edge of the ceiling. We had some trim just like that in our apartment in the city."

"Well, they said the place was somewhere right here in Riverhurst," Kate reminded us. "There are no apartments in Riverhurst. Besides, every old building has that kind of trim."

"I don't think they want people to guess," she said. "I think the whole thing's a publicity stunt."

"If any of you fans out there have any ideas, call

1-800 BOODLES." It was Russell Gartner again. "Keep watching this station for a second video clue. And stop by the Record Emporium for our album and a free poster of Boodles, signed by yours truly."

"If the other clues are anything like this one, I'll never get to be a video star," Stephanie declared with a sigh. "I'll just have to impress Michael on stage at school." She switched off the TV. "Let's practice our scenes, Patti. Kate and Lauren can read some of the parts for us. Okay?"

"Where do you want to do it?" Kate said to Patti.

"Uh — I don't know . . ." Patti replied. She looked so freaked out about just *practicing* that I couldn't imagine her making it through the tryout.

"Are you sure you want to be in the play?" I asked her again.

"Of course she does," Stephanie answered. "It's really going to be fun, right, Patti? Maybe we should practice in the attic."

The Jenkinses' house has a low attic above the second floor. Sometimes we dance up there — there's plenty of open space, and we can make a lot of noise without bothering Patti's parents.

"That's a good idea," Kate said. "Have you decided which part you're trying out for, Stephanie?"

We started up the stairs.

"Laura," Stephanie replied.

Laura is the star of *The Woman in Blue*. She's a beautiful heiress whose hand in marriage has been promised to Sir Monty. Sir Monty is the villain in the story, and Laura doesn't love him. She loves Alex Doright, a penniless art teacher.

"What about you, Patti?" I asked.

"Stephanie thought I might be good as Sara," she said.

Sara is Laura's cousin. She doesn't have much money, and nothing really happens to her. On the other hand, she doesn't have too much to say.

On the second floor, the door to Horace's room was open a crack, but the lights were off and the boys were quiet. Kate headed for the flight of stairs leading to the attic.

"Wait a second — we need our scripts," Stephanie reminded her.

We walked back down the hall to Patti's room, where we'd left our overnight stuff. Patti pulled her copy of the script out of a drawer in her desk. Kate and I had folded ours up and stuffed them into our backpacks. Stephanie unzipped her canvas tote and reached into it for her script.

"Eeeeeeeeeeeah!" she screamed at the top of her lungs.

"What is it?" Kate yelled. Patti, Kate, and I stared as Stephanie scrambled backward so fast she knocked a lamp over.

"There's — there's — something hairy in my tote!" Stephanie gasped. "It — it *moved!*"

"Hairy?" Patti and I edged away, but Kate moved closer to the tote. She leaned forward. With one finger, she pulled the flap open a little.

"It's a rat!" she shrieked.

"A rat!" Patti, Stephanie, and I screeched. We jumped up on Patti's bed. Kate climbed onto the desk chair.

As we peered at Stephanie's tote, a pink nose appeared over the side of the flap.

"Eeeeeee!" we squealed. The three of us huddled together in the middle of the bed.

The pink nose pointed in our direction and wiggled for a second. It was followed by two beady brown eyes, round, pinkish ears —

"It *is* a rat!" Stephanie whispered.

"Girls? What's going on in there?" Mr. Jenkins called out. Patti's father had been reading in his bedroom. We could hear him racing down the hall, but not one of us said a word. We were absolutely frozen, watching the rat.

It kind of oozed out of Stephanie's tote and onto

the floor. It was dark brown, but it had creepy little pink feet and a slick pink tail. The rat sniffed the air. Then it crept across the rug toward the bed.

"What if it crawls up the bedspread?" Stephanie squeaked.

The rat didn't have the chance. Mr. Jenkins bounded through the door to Patti's room, and the rat retreated in a hurry — under the bed we were standing on.

"Daddy — there's an enormous rat under my bed!" Patti barely managed to explain.

"A rat?" Mr. Jenkins said.

"It was inside my tote. I actually touched it!" Stephanie shivered.

Mr. Jenkins got down on his hands and knees to look under Patti's bed. "I see it," he said. "It's pressed against the back wall."

He climbed to his feet. In an unusually loud voice, he announced, "A good whack with a broom handle should take care of the rat — permanently. Stay where you are, girls. I'll just run downstairs — "

Lester burst into Patti's room. "No! You're not whacking my rat with any old broom!"

Chapter 6

"*Your* rat! Just as I thought!" said Mr. Jenkins. "Lester, how did this rat get into Stephanie's tote?"

"I brought Ratenstein from home in my suitcase, because I didn't want him to be alone all weekend," Lester answered. "I thought I'd surprise the girls a little. No big deal."

"No big deal!" I'd never seen Patti look so mad. She stalked across the bed, her fists clenched. Mild-mannered Patti Jenkins was ready to punch Lester in the nose!

"Hold on, Patti," her father said. "I'll take care of this."

"Daddy, he's absolutely ruining my sleepover!" Patti practically shouted.

"Good!" Stephanie cried. "Remember this an-

51

ger. It will help when you're acting."

Mr. Jenkins stared at Stephanie for a moment, then grabbed Lester's arm, ready to march him out of the room. "Let's go," he said grimly.

"My rat, Uncle Phil!" Lester protested.

"Let him take his rat!"

"Get it — fast!" Mr. Jenkins told Lester.

Lester lay down on the floor with his head under Patti's bed. "Here, Ratenstein — here, Ratty — some treats for you. . . ." Lester scrunched under the bed up to his shoulders. "Got you!" he exclaimed in a muffled voice.

Stephanie, Patti, and I backed away from the edge of the bed as Lester wriggled out. When he stood up, Ratenstein was squirming in his hand, pink feet waving in the air, slick pink tail thrashing back and forth.

"Eeeee-uuuuu!" Stephanie shivered again.

"Ick!" said Kate from her perch on the desk chair.

Lester waved Ratenstein toward us.

"Lester, that will do!" Mr. Jenkins growled. "Keep this up, and you won't watch television again until you're a very old man! Take your rat to your room and keep it there. I don't want to see it — or you — again tonight!"

Lester waited until Mr. Jenkins had turned around, and then he stuck out his tongue at us. "Dumb girls!" he mouthed, before he disappeared down the hall with Ratenstein clinging to the shoulder of his pajamas.

Patti, Stephanie, and I jumped down from the bed.

Kate stepped off the chair. "Thanks, Mr. Jenkins. That was gross!"

"Lester won't bother you again," Mr. Jenkins assured us.

Mrs. Jenkins got home from her meeting just about a minute later. "I'm exhausted — I'm going straight to bed," she told us when she came upstairs. "I left a carton of fudge ripple ice cream in the freezer, and a big bag of fresh chocolate chunk cookies on the table. Don't stay up too late."

"We won't, Mom," Patti promised.

We carried out scripts down the hall to the stairs that led to the attic. There wasn't a sound coming from Horace's room.

"I hope they're asleep," Patti whispered.

"I hope Ratenstein's asleep," Stephanie added.

The attic stairs are behind a door, just across the hall from Horace's room. The stairs are steep and narrow, and low — Patti and I have to stoop a little as we walk up. Then you step out into one big space with a pointed ceiling and criss-crossing rafters that stretch across the whole top of the Jenkinses' house. The windows are round, like portholes on a boat. Patti switched on the light.

"We'd better get right to work," Stephanie said. "Let's do Scene 2 — the one where Laura and Sara are waiting for Alex to give them a drawing lesson. I'm Laura, and Patti's Sara."

"And I'm directing, so that leaves Lauren to be Alex Doright," said Kate.

"Thanks a lot," I said.

"Don't mention it." Kate grinned at me. "Okay — Laura is supposed to be sketching Sara. Patti, you're posing for a picture. Stand near the wall and look interested. Stephanie, sit on that stool and pretend to be drawing."

Patti and Stephanie took their places.

"Sara, go ahead," Kate said.

Not a word from Patti.

"Sara? Patti? Read the first line, please," Kate directed.

Patti looked petrified.

"Patti!" Stephanie/Laura said impatiently.

"Er. A-hem." Patti cleared her throat and shuffled her feet. "Yes." She looked down at her script. "Have . . . you almost . . . finished, Laura . . . dear."

Patti managed to get through the sentence, but I could barely hear her, and I wasn't standing very far away.

Then Stephanie read her lines. "Not quite. How *enchanting* you look, cousin Sara," she trilled. "I hope Mr. Doright will be pleased." She spoke clearly, her voice carried, and she sounded kind of grown-up. Stephanie was good.

We waited for Patti to read the next line. She still hadn't moved — I think she was forgetting to breathe.

"Patti!" Stephanie hissed.

"Um. Er. I fear, Laura . . . that Mr. Doright's . . . attention . . . to you is . . . more than one . . . might expect from . . . the usual drawing . . . teacher."

Patti put so many spaces between the words that it was hard to tell where the sentence began and where it ended.

"If she doesn't get a whole lot better, fast, her tryout is going to be awful," I whispered in Kate's ear.

Kate nodded. "Good, Patti," she said encouragingly.

"Hush, you shall make me blush," Stephanie was saying with a shy smile — *Laura's* shy smile, since Stephanie is definitely not shy.

"C-Cupid has . . . p-pierced your . . . heart with . . . a paintbrush," Patti stammered.

Stephanie fluttered her hand in the air. "If he has, it has caused me no pain."

"Okay, Alex." Kate nudged me forward.

"What a lovely scene," I said in a deep voice.

Kate snickered. "You sound like Santa Claus, Lauren."

"Do you want me to be Alex, or not?" I muttered.

"Sorry — go ahead," the director said.

"What a lovely scene," I said in Alex's voice. In a stage whisper, he added to the audience, "There is the lady who holds my heart, Miss Laura Knickerbocker. But how could I ever hope to win her love? I'm but a penniless drawing teacher."

"Did you speak, Mr. Doright?" said Stephanie/ Laura very sweetly.

"Dear Miss Knickerbocker, I see you are practicing your sketching. Good, good."

No one spoke for a minute.

"Patti," Kate finally said.

Patti jumped. "Me?" she squeaked. "Oh. Er. We

56

. . . missed you . . . I lost my place — sorry."

"At breakfast, Mr. Doright!" Stephanie growled through her teeth.

The longer we rehearsed, the worse Patti got. It was pitiful. Finally, I couldn't stand it any longer. "What about taking a break? I'd love some chocolate chunk cookies and ice cream."

"Oh — sure!" Patti cheered up immediately. "Let's go to the kitchen."

She led the way down the narrow staircase. When we got to the bottom, the small door to the second floor hall was closed.

"I don't remember closing the door," Kate said, "and I was the last one up."

Patti reached for the knob and tried to turn it. "I think it's stuck," she said. "You know these old doors — want to help me, Lauren?"

I twisted the knob while Patti pushed against the door. It didn't budge.

"Let me take a look," Kate ordered. She squeezed past Patti and me and leaned close to the knob while she jiggled it. Finally she straightened up. "You know what I think?" she said. "I think Lester has struck again. He's locked us in."

"You're kidding!" said Stephanie. "Let me try it."

She rattled and pulled at the knob, too, but her luck wasn't any better. "We're locked in," she said.

"That little creep!" Patti said in a strangled voice. "I'm going to kill him!"

"We have to get out first — what if we bang on the door and yell?" Kate suggested.

"The door is really thick, and my parents' bedroom is at the other end of the hall. Plus their door is closed," said Patti bitterly.

"So basically the only people who might hear us are Lester and Horace," I summed up.

"And Lester won't unlock the door or let Horace unlock it," said Stephanie.

"I'm going to give it a shot, anyway." Kate started kicking the door and shouting "Let us out!" We all took turns, until our feet hurt and our throats were sore, but nobody came.

"This is awful!" Patti moaned. "I bet this is the worst sleepover any of you has ever been at. We'll have to stay up here all night long, with no snacks, nothing to drink. . . ."

"It's getting kind of cool," Stephanie said, hugging herself.

"And no heat!" Patti wailed.

"We won't have to stay up here," I said. "We can climb out a window."

"On the third floor?" Stephanie shrieked. "Are you crazy, Lauren?"

I shook my head. "Isn't that big chestnut tree right next to the house?"

Patti nodded. "On this side." She unlatched a window.

I pushed it open and looked out. I could touch some thick branches without even stretching. "We can do it," I said.

"Maybe you and Patti can," said Kate. "My legs are too short — I'm staying here."

"So am I," said Stephanie.

Patti was already crawling through the window. "It's my sleepover and my rotten cousin," she said. "I'll climb down and squeeze through the kitchen window. I'll get you out of here in no time."

"And then we'll all kill Lester," said Stephanie.

"Wait a minute, Patti. It's really dark. What if you slip?" Kate said.

"I've climbed this tree lots of times," Patti told her. "I could probably climb it blindfolded." Patti is shy, but she's not a chicken.

While we hung onto one of her arms, Patti stepped into the chestnut tree and grabbed a branch with her other hand.

"Patti, be careful."

"Go slowly."

"Are you okay?"

"I'm fine," Patti said from inside the tree. "There are so many branches, it's as easy as walking down a ladder."

It was so dark out that we couldn't see a thing. We could hear her for a little while, stepping down from branch to branch. Then we didn't hear anything. I leaned as far out of the window as I could.

"Patti?" I called softly.

"I'm on the ground," she called back. "See you in a minute."

I'd barely pulled my head back inside when a siren went off! It was so loud that we had to shout to hear ourselves.

"Are we near a firehouse?" Kate yelled.

"What? You think the house is on fire? I'm going out that window!" Stephanie screeched.

Kate and I pulled her away from it.

"I don't think it's the fire department siren," I shouted.

"It sounds almost as though it's inside the house," Kate bellowed.

"What's that light?" Stephanie screamed, pointing straight up.

A bright light streaked through a round window

and across the attic ceiling . . . again . . . and again
. . . and again. The three of us peered out the window
to see a flashing light on the roof of . . .

"A police car!" Kate gasped.

It pulled up outside the Jenkinses' house, and
two policemen jumped out.

The siren stopped as suddenly as it had begun.

"Why are the police here?" Stephanie shouted
into the quiet. "What if something's happened to
Patti?"

Kate and I looked at each other, then all three
of us raced down the narrow stairs and started bang-
ing on the closed door. There was a loud click on
the other side of the door — and we were free! We
saw the back of Lester's pajamas as he dashed across
the hall into Horace's room and slammed the door
shut.

"We'll get him later," Kate said.

The three of us flew down the second flight of
stairs. All the lights were blazing on the first floor.
There were voices coming from the kitchen. We
charged through the door in time to hear Mr. Jenkins
say, "The burglar alarm came with the house. I haven't
turned it on since we moved in. I can't understand
how it happened — a short in the wires, maybe?"

"And I can't understand what a ten-year-old girl

61

was doing climbing through a kitchen window in the middle of the night," Officer Warner said.

"Patti, would you like to explain to all of us?" her father said sternly.

"I'm having a sleepover," Patti began in her soft voice. "Stephanie Green, Kate Beekman, Lauren Hunter, and I were in the attic, practicing for the fifth-grade play when" — her voice got a lot louder — "my creepy cousin Lester locked us in! No one heard us shouting, and we didn't want to be stuck up there all night, so I climbed out a window. . . ."

"You did *what*?" her mother exclaimed. "Oh, Patti — you could have hurt yourself badly!"

"It was fine, Mom — I climbed down the old chestnut tree. But when I tried to crawl through the kitchen window, the alarm went off."

"It was so loud we heard it on the next block and drove right over here," said the other officer. "We thought it was a break-in."

"Where are the switches to the alarm system?" Officer Warner asked.

"At the top of the stairs." Mrs. Jenkins led the policemen through the living room and up the stairs to the second floor.

I'd never noticed the switches before. They were low on the wall, and the word "ALARM" was printed just above them. And they were very close to the door of Horace's room.

"You know what I think?" Kate whispered to me. "I think — "

"Lester strikes again!" Patti said to her father.

Chapter
7

"Patti, this wins hands down as the most exciting sleepover we've ever had," Kate said. "We almost get karate-chopped in your living room, then Lauren and Stephanie eat hot-pepper pizza and drink olive oil. Then we get locked in the attic — "

"Don't forget Ratenstein," I interrupted.

"Oh, yeah — then we're attacked by a giant rat. Then you risk your life climbing out a third-floor window, and you set off a burglar alarm. . . ."

"And the police come, and you practically get arrested!" Stephanie finished.

"Of course, that doesn't necessarily mean that we want Lester at all of our sleepovers," Kate added.

We all giggled. Officer Warner and his partner had left, and Mr. and Mrs. Jenkins had gone up to bed. We were too keyed-up to go to sleep yet and were lounging around the living room.

"How about that ice cream?" I suggested.

Patti brought out the whole container of fudge ripple, the bag of chocolate chunk cookies, and sodas for everybody. Stephanie switched on the TV and turned to Video Trax. We hadn't been watching long when Russell Gartner popped up again.

"Hey, guys and gals! After a whole week of Video Clue Number One, nobody's even come close to guessing the location for our premiere video," he said. "Since you're so bad, and we're so good, we're going to give you another chance. Ready? Here's the second clue."

"Video Clue #2 — Boodles" flashed on the screen. We were back in the polka-dotted room, but this time Russell Gartner and a couple of other spiky-haired guys were leaning out a window. It was night. Below them was a sidewalk, and some round bushes, and a street with dark trees on either side of it. As the camera moved across the scene, a fuzzy gray blob floated across the bottom of the screen.

"Does it look like anyplace you know?" Patti asked. She hasn't really been in Riverhurst long enough to recognize many places.

"Practically every street in Riverhurst looks like

65

that," Stephanie said, disgusted. "Kate's right — it's just a publicity stunt. They don't really want anybody to guess." She stood up. "Michael Pastore will just have to see me on stage — let's go rehearse some more."

"I think we've all had enough for one night," Kate said firmly.

Patti looked very grateful. But Stephanie made Patti rehearse the next afternoon, and Sunday and Monday, too.

The auditions for *The Woman in Blue* were Wednesday afternoon after school. Practically everyone in fifth grade was in the gym, including the teachers. I was in the big group getting started on the sets. Ms. Gilberto, the art teacher, and two or three people in the fifth grade who can draw were sketching in outlines for things like windows and curtains and bookshelves. The rest of us were filling them in with paint, trying to stay inside the lines.

Then Mr. Coulter boomed out, "Let's get started." All eyes went to the stage. "I need a Laura, a Sara, and an Alex," Mr. Coulter said. He read from the list: "Jenny Carlin, Jane Sykes, and Robert Ellwanger — take your places on stage."

Sally Mason, another girl from 5B, and I were sharing a can of green paint. "Robert Ellwanger as

Alex?" Sally groaned. "He has to be the nerdiest boy in school!"

Robert was terrible, and Jenny Carlin wasn't much better as Laura — she flapped her arms around and shrieked her lines. Kate was sitting next to Mr. Coulter in a row of chairs in front of the stage. She turned around and rolled her eyes at me about Jenny Carlin.

Jane Sykes was okay as Sara, but the other two were such turkeys that she kind of got lost.

"Awful!" said Sally. "At least I *know* I'm not an actor."

"Thank you, Robert and Jenny. Thank you, Jane," Mr. Coulter said. "Let's try a scene with another Laura, and Sir Monty. Um — Betsy Chalfin and Mark Freedman."

"All-l-l-l right, Mark!" Tommy Brown called from the back of the gym.

Mark was great. When he twirled his imaginary mustache and drawled, "Our wedding date draws near," then kissed Betsy/Laura's hand, a bunch of kids applauded. But Betsy was too mousy for Laura — Stephanie didn't have much competition there.

I looked around the gym and spotted Kathy Simons working on a sketch with Kyle Hubbard and another boy. I expected to find her latched onto Michael, but I didn't see Michael anywhere. Stephanie and Patti were huddled together not far from the stage. Stephanie was whispering a mile a minute, probably giving Patti more instructions about how to act. They didn't have long to wait. Mr. Coulter called them next.

"We'll try the Laura, Sara, and Alex scene again," he said. "This time, Stephanie Green will be Laura, Patti Jenkins, Sara, and . . . Michael Pastore, Alex Doright."

Michael Pastore? I didn't even know he'd signed up on the list!

Stephanie didn't either. She was practically skipping up the steps to the stage until she heard his name. Then she stopped dead and stared at Mr. Coulter. Patti bumped right into her, which made several kids giggle.

"Michael? Are you here?" Mr. Coulter called out.

"Yes, sir — sorry I'm late." Michael had slipped into the gym through the side door.

"Take your places, please," said Mr. Coulter.

Out of the corner of my eye, I saw Kathy Simons moving closer. Stephanie looked like a sleepwalker as she crossed the stage and sat down on the stool. Patti nodded and smiled at her.

"Please begin, Sara," said Mr. Coulter.

Patti was holding her script, but Stephanie had made her rehearse so many times that she didn't have to look at it.

"Have you almost finished, Laura, dear?" Patti said her first line straight out, without fumbling or stammering. She didn't have any trouble, because she was worried about poor Stephanie and wasn't thinking about herself.

It was Stephanie who was frozen. She stared offstage, where Michael Pastore was waiting to walk on.

"Stephanie?" Mr. Coulter said.

Stephanie had memorized her lines days before — she hadn't even bothered to bring a script. Now she couldn't remember anything.

"Uh . . . uh . . ." she mumbled.

"Not quite. How enchanting . . ." Mr. Coulter prompted her.

"Not quite. . . . How enchanting?" Stephanie repeated, without any expression at all.

"I thought Stephanie would be good," Sally Mason said to me.

"She is good," I said. "Usually."

"Kate, please hand Stephanie a copy of the script," Mr. Coulter said.

But that didn't help. Stephanie didn't seem to

be able to find her place. When Michael walked onstage, it got even worse. Stephanie's voice shook, and I could hardly hear her.

Finally Mr. Coulter broke in. "I'd like to try the same scene again, but with Patti as Laura, and Stephanie as Sara."

"I — I'm not feeling very well," Stephanie blurted out, just before she ran down the stage steps and out the side door.

"Be right back," I said to Sally Mason. I put down my paintbrush and hurried after Stephanie.

She was halfway across the lawn before I caught up with her, heading for the bike rack. She looked as though she were about to cry.

"I've never gotten stage fright before. But I took one look at Michael," Stephanie said, "and I forgot *everything*. Really made a great impression on him, didn't I?"

"It wasn't so bad," I said.

"It was awful." Stephanie tried to smile. "Poor Patti. I made her go through all this for nothing."

She climbed on her bike. "See you tomorrow, Lauren."

By the time I got back to the gym, Tracy Osner as Laura, Henry Larkin as Sir Monty, and Christy Soames as the maid were on stage.

"Patti Jenkins was really good as Laura," Sally Mason reported. "Does Michael Pastore like her?"

Uh-oh! I thought. "Not that I know of," I said. "Why?"

"He smiled at her the whole time." Sally added a dab of paint to a window frame. "And I don't think he was acting."

Chapter
8

Stephanie had pulled herself together by the next morning. The four of us rode our bikes to school, as usual, and the only thing Stephanie said about the play was to Patti: "Listen, I know you didn't want to try out — and I'm sorry I made you do it."

Lunch was okay, too. Michael Pastore and Kyle and some of the other boys ate way over on the other side of the cafeteria. But Mrs. Mead made an announcement that afternoon, just before she dismissed us.

"Class, the four fifth-grade teachers and Mr. Coulter have discussed yesterday's auditions, and we've come up with the cast for this year's play, *The Woman in Blue.*" Mrs. Mead smiled broadly. "Two members of the cast are also members of our room, 5B. The part of the villain, Sir Monty, will be played by . . . Mark Freedman!"

Everyone started clapping, and Mark stood up to take a bow.

When he'd sat down again, Mrs. Mead went on: "We also have in our class the student who will be playing the part of Laura . . ."

I took a quick look around the room. Who? Surely not Jenny Carlin!

". . . Patti Jenkins!"

Stephanie whirled around in her seat to stare open-mouthed at Patti, who was turning a bright red as everyone applauded.

"Just great!" Kate murmured to me.

"The other members of the cast," said Mrs. Mead, "are Barbara Paulson as Sara, Karen Sims as Margaret the maid, Michael Pastore as Alex Doright. . . ."

I'm sure not one of the four of us heard anything else after that. When the bell finally rang, we trooped out in a daze. That's when the final blow fell. Michael Pastore was hanging around in the hall, just outside the door to 5B. When he saw Patti, his face broke into a big smile.

"Hey, Patti!" Michael said. "Congratulations! I

thought maybe we could go over a couple of our scenes together, if you don't have to get home right away."

Stephanie marched past him without looking to the left or to the right.

"Wait up, Stephanie!" Kate called.

But Stephanie jumped on her bike and pedaled furiously away.

I called her at home that evening. "Hi, Stephanie," I said. "I just want to remind you that the sleepover's at my house tomorrow."

"Is Patti going?" she asked after a moment or two.

"I'm sure she is," I said carefully.

"Then I'm not." Stephanie hung up.

"This is ridiculous!" Patti wailed when I called her. "I only tried out for the dumb play because Stephanie begged me to. I never wanted to be in it, and I *still* don't. And Michael's a nice boy, but I don't *like* him — he's too *short!*"

"I know that, and you know that, and Stephanie *should* know that," I said, "but she's too upset right now to make any sense."

Stephanie didn't show up on her bike to ride to school with us the next morning, and neither did Patti. We found out later that Stephanie had ridden

74

the school bus because she didn't want to see Patti, and Patti had asked her mother to drive her to school because she didn't want to upset Stephanie.

Kate and I pedaled slowly up the hill and coasted down the other side toward Riverhurst Elementary.

"So — is this the end of the Sleepover Friends?" I said gloomily.

Kate shook her head. "I'm sure Stephanie will calm down."

I wasn't so sure. At lunch, Stephanie filled her tray, glared at all three of us, and went to sit with Jenny Carlin, whom she knows I can't stand. After school, Stephanie jumped on the bus before we even had a chance to say goodbye.

By the time Patti and Kate got to my house for the sleepover that night, we were all feeling pretty discouraged.

"What if I told Stephanie I won't be in the play?" Patti said.

"The teachers would be really annoyed with you," Kate replied. "Besides, nothing changes the fact that you were picked for the part."

"Or that Michael likes you," I added.

We were sitting in the den with the television on and the sound turned down. My mom stuck her head around the door. "Roger's going for Chinese food. Does anyone have any special requests?"

We all shook our heads. "I'm not really hungry," I said.

"Lauren's not hungry?" It was Roger. "Is she dead?"

"Ha, ha." I stuck my tongue out at him.

"Where's Stephanie?" he asked, looking around the room.

"Don't ask," my mother mumbled, pulling him into the hall.

"Requests!" Patti said. "I think your mom said something about requests!"

"Patti, what are you talking about?" Kate asked.

"What if we dedicate a song to Stephanie on WBRM tonight? Something about friendship, or being sorry, or something."

"Too embarrassing — all the kids who are listening will know we're fighting, and why," I said.

"Why don't we just call Stephanie up?" Kate asked.

"She probably won't talk to us," I replied. But I went to the phone and dialed her number.

Mrs. Green answered. "Why, hello, Lauren."

"May I speak to Stephanie, please?"

Mrs. Green lowered her voice. "I'm afraid she

doesn't feel like talking right now, Lauren. Why don't you try her tomorrow?''

I barely tasted the sweet-and-sour pork Roger brought back from Szechuan Empire. We were watching Video Trax and trying to think of what to do when Russell Gartner came on the screen.

''Listen up out there!'' he said, running his fingers through his short blond hair. ''We're running out of time. It's been two weeks, and no one has guessed the location of our video. Don't you want to be stars?''

''Turn that clown off!'' Kate snapped. ''Let's go upstairs.''

We tried a few games of Mad Libs, but it was depressing: we kept coming up with words like *sad*, *gloomy*, *crying*, *angry*, and *fight*.

''What time is it?'' Patti asked. ''Maybe we should just go to bed.''

''At eleven o'clock?'' I said. ''At a sleepover?''

So Kate started telling us a long and complicated ghost story she'd heard at summer camp. My parents were asleep, Roger was out with friends, and the house was absolutely quiet. Kate was getting to the part of the story where the ghost appears to the young married couple and cries, ''Give me back my head-d-d . . . give me back my he-e-ead!"

Patti shivered. "I can almost hear it moaning, can't you?" she whispered to me.

I *did* hear something moaning. But was I going to say so and have Kate tell me that my imagination was running away with me again? No way!

Luckily, Kate heard it herself. "Listen!" she said suddenly. "What's that?"

It wasn't exactly a moan — more like a creepy, whining sound.

"It sounds like it's coming from the back of the house," she decided.

We tiptoed down the hall to the spare room and opened the window. There it was again — maybe it was a moan after all.

"Could it be Bullwinkle?" Kate asked me in a low voice.

Bullwinkle is Roger's dog. He's mostly New-foundland, he weighs one hundred and thirty pounds, and when he's standing up on his hind legs, he's five feet tall. Bullwinkle is older than I am, and he stills thinks he's a puppy.

I shook my head. "Bullwinkle is locked up in the garage."

Patti pointed a shaky finger. "Look — isn't that the old McBride house?"

"You were right, Lauren — there *is* a light on at the McBride house," Kate said.

A bright light streamed through the windows on one side of the second floor. "And I think that's where the sound is coming from," I said.

"I'm sure there's a logical explanation. I'm going to investigate." Kate headed for the stairs.

"Wait!" I hissed. "I think we should tell my dad. . . ."

But Kate was already halfway down. We crept through the house to the kitchen and out the back door. We stood for a minute on the back steps. The whining, moaning sound grew louder.

"Shouldn't we take a flashlight?" Patti's voice trembled.

"No — we'd give ourselves away!" Kate whispered.

"Well, I'm taking some protection," I said.

"Like what?" said Kate.

"Bullwinkle!"

Kate snickered, but she waited for me to open the garage door and snap on Bullwinkle's leash.

Bullwinkle was so excited to get out of the garage that he almost pulled me over. He galloped across the driveway and flung himself on Kate and then licked Patti's face.

"You have to make him be quiet, Lauren!" Kate whispered.

I wrapped an arm around Bullwinkle's neck and leaned on him, hard. Patti and I followed Kate through the hedge that separates my yard from the backyard of the McBride house.

We sneaked around the house to stand under the lighted windows. The moaning sound had stopped, but we could hear soft, thumping noises coming from upstairs.

"I wish we could see in!" Kate whispered.

"I think we should call the police, don't you, Lauren?" said Patti.

All of a sudden, Bullwinkle lunged away from me, jerking the leash out of my hand.

"Grab him!" Kate said, throwing herself at him. But it was too late.

"RRRUFFFF!" Bullwinkle bounded around the McBride house before we could stop him. There was a crash. Then a weak voice called out, "Help!"

The three of us raced into the front yard to find Bullwinkle standing with his front paws on a man's chest.

"Help!" the man said again, trying to catch his breath as Bullwinkle gave his nose a swipe with his long, pink tongue.

The dim glow from the streetlamp fell on the man's face and short, spiky blond hair.

"RUSSELL GARTNER!" Kate, Patti, and I shrieked.

He was lying next to the gray blob I'd noticed at the bottom of the screen in Video Clue Number Two — the old birdbath. And the whining noise we'd heard? It had been the electric guitar Russell was still clutching!

"This is where Boodles is shooting the video!" I yelled.

"Will you please get this ox off of me?" wheezed Russell Gartner.

We called Stephanie early the next morning. "Mrs. Green, it's Lauren again," I said. "Will Stephanie talk to us now?" Mrs. Green was quiet for a moment.

"Let me check," she replied.

"Would you please tell her we're all going to be in the video?"

"The video?"

"Yes — she'll know what I mean."

"All right." Mrs. Green put the phone down. I heard the sound of footsteps walking down the hall to Stephanie's room, then the murmur of voices. Suddenly there was a shriek and, "You're kidding!"

I grinned and did the thumbs-up sign at Kate and Patti. "That got her all right. She's coming."

Stephanie raced to the phone. "Lauren?" she said breathlessly. "You guessed the video?"

"Yep — they're shooting it in the old McBride house, which just happens to belong to Russell Gartner's cousin."

"And all *four* of us are in it?"

"The Sleepover Friends are the new Boodles back-up group."

"Far out!" said Stephanie. "Don't move — I'll be right over. We have to practice some steps."

Chapter
9

Making a video is a lot more work than it looks. On Sunday afternoon, all four of the Sleepover Friends were in the black-and-white polka-dotted room: Kate, Patti, Stephanie, and me. We weren't the only ones in the room, of course. There was also Russell Gartner, and Kevin Dawson, and David Berners — Boodles. Also the director of the video, the cameraman, the assistant director, the assistant cameraman, the sound man, the lights man, even Bullwinkle — Russell said he fit in with the color scheme, because he has black fur.

Kate was wearing black jeans and a red-and-white sweatshirt, Patti had on a red-and-black T-shirt with white sweatpants, and I was wearing red sweatpants and a black-and-white sweatshirt. Stephanie was wearing her black-and-white jumpsuit and dangly red earrings.

"Ready?" said the director.

We all nodded.

"Roll sound," said the assistant director. "Roll camera."

The camera started to whir.

As the assistant cameraman held up the slate with numbers written on it, Stephanie turned to us with a big grin. "Stars!" she said.

"Scene one, take one," said the assistant cameraman.

"And action!" said the director.

Russell and Kevin played a couple of licks on their guitars, David Berners pounded on the drums, and the black-and-white spotted room in the old McBride house filled with the sound of Boodles singing, "I've Gone Dotty Over You." The four of us started to dance . . . and Bullwinkle started to howl! I've never been so embarrassed!

"Cut . . . cut!" shouted the director.

Everything stopped. The director shook his head. "The dog has to go," he said.

And Bullwinkle looked so cute — I'd even bought him a new red collar. I led him home and closed him up in the garage.

When I got back, we took it from the top. On scene one, take two, Patti got out of step in her dancing. Scene one, take three, Russell bumped into Kevin, who dropped his guitar. Scene two, take one, the camera jammed. A couple of times *Stephanie* asked for a retake: "I think we can do it better, don't you?" she said to us. Both times, the director said he didn't think so.

By scene three, take five, Kate was ready to quit. "*I'll* go dotty if I hear 'I've Gone Dotty Over You' one more time," she growled.

We were waiting for the cameraman to reload. "Bullwinkle was right," I whispered to Kate. Boodles were loud — but they weren't any good.

"If they were any good, would they be shooting a video in the old McBride house?" Kate asked.

"Just think of Stephanie," Patti whispered. She nodded toward Stephanie, who was going over her steps in the corner. "She's working so hard — for Michael."

"We're doing this for Stephanie," I repeated.

Anyway, they kept us going until the director announced at last, "It's a wrap!"

We got back to my house half-deaf, with blisters on our feet and four free, autographed posters of Boodles.

"These posters'll be worth five cents in a year or two," Kate said. "The longer Boodles played, the worse they got!" she groaned with her fingers in her ears. "I bet they never make it to Video Trax!"

"Of course they will," I said, looking at Stephanie. "And Michael will love it."

"Michael?" asked Stephanie. She sounded as though she'd never heard of him.

"Michael Pastore?" I reminded her.

"Oh, *that* Michael," she said. "I think Russell Gartner's a lot cuter, don't you?"

APPLE®PAPERBACKS

More books you'll love, filled with mystery, adventure, friendship, and fun!

NEW APPLE TITLES

☐ 40284-6	**Christina's Ghost**	Betty Ren Wright	$2.50
☐ 41839-4	**A Ghost in the Window**	Betty Ren Wright	$2.50
☐ 41794-0	**Katie and Those Boys**	Martha Tolles	$2.50
☐ 40565-9	**Secret Agents Four**	Donald J. Sobol	$2.50
☐ 40554-3	**Sixth Grade Sleepover**	Eve Bunting	$2.50
☐ 40419-9	**When the Dolls Woke**	Marjorie Filley Stover	$2.50

BEST SELLING APPLE TITLES

☐ 41042-3	**The Dollhouse Murders**	Betty Ren Wright	$2.50
☐ 42319-3	**The Friendship Pact**	Susan Beth Pfeffer	$2.75
☐ 40755-4	**Ghosts Beneath Our Feet**	Betty Ren Wright	$2.50
☐ 40605-1	**Help! I'm a Prisoner in the Library**	Eth Clifford	$2.50
☐ 40724-4	**Katie's Baby-sitting Job**	Martha Tolles	$2.50
☐ 40494-6	**The Little Gymnast**	Sheila Haigh	$2.50
☐ 40283-8	**Me and Katie (The Pest)**	Ann M. Martin	$2.50
☐ 42316-9	**Nothing's Fair in Fifth Grade**	Barthe DeClements	$2.75
☐ 40607-8	**Secrets in the Attic**	Carol Beach York	$2.50
☐ 40180-7	**Sixth Grade Can Really Kill You**	Barthe DeClements	$2.50
☐ 41118-7	**Tough-luck Karen**	Johanna Hurwitz	$2.50
☐ 42326-6	**Veronica the Show-off**	Nancy K. Robinson	$2.75
☐ 42374-6	**Who's Reading Darci's Diary?**	Martha Tolles	$2.75

Available wherever you buy books...or use the coupon below.